RED ACES
BY

Edgar Wallace

FOREWORD

Edgar Wallace was a British author who is best known for creating King Kong. Wallace was a very prolific writer despite his sudden death at age 56. In total Wallace is credited with over 170 novels, almost 1,000 short stories, and 18 stage plays. Wallace's works have been turned into well over 100 films.

Red Aces

First published in The Thriller magazine, February 9, 1929

I. — THE THREAT

WHEN a young man is very much in love with a most attractive girl he is apt to endow her with qualities and virtues which no human being has ever possessed. Yet at rare and painful intervals there enter into his soul certain wild suspicions, and in these moments he is inclined to consider the possibility that she may be guilty of the basest treachery and double dealing.

Everybody knew that Kenneth McKay was desperately in love. They knew it at the bank where he spent his days in counting other people's money, and a considerable amount of his lunch hour writing impassioned and ill-spelt letters to Margot Lynn. His taciturn father, brooding over his vanished fortune in his gaunt riverside house at Marlow, may have employed the few moments he gave to the consideration of other people's troubles in consideration of his son's new interest. Probably he did not, for George McKay was entirely self-centred and had little thought but for the folly which had dissipated the money he had accumulated with such care, and the development of fantastical schemes for its recovery.

Kenneth went over to Beaconsfield every morning on his noisy motorbike and came back every night, sometimes very late, because Margot lived in London; they dined together at the cheaper restaurants and sometimes saw a film. Kenneth was a member of an inexpensive London club which sheltered at least one sympathetic soul. Except for Rufus Machfield, the confidant in question, he had no friends.

'And let me advise you not to make any here,' said Rufus.

He was a military-looking man of forty-five, and most people found him rather a bore, for the views which he expressed so vehemently, on all subjects from politics to religion, which are the opposite ends of the ethical pole, he had acquired that morning from the leading article of his favourite daily. Yet he was a genial person—a likeable man.

He had a luxurious flat in Park Lane, a French valet, a Bentley and no useful occupation.

'The Leffingham Club is cheap.' he said, 'the food's not bad and it's near Piccadilly. Against that you have the fact that almost anybody who hasn't been to prison can become a member—'

'The fact that I'm a member—' began Ken.

'You're a gentleman and a public school man,' interrupted Mr Machfield sonorously. 'You're not rich, I admit—'

'Even I admit that,' said Ken, rubbing his untidy hair.

Kenneth was tall, athletic, as good-looking as a young man need be, or can be without losing his head about his face. He had called at the Leffingham that evening especially to see Rufus and confide his worries. And his worries were enormous. He looked haggard and ill: Mr Machfield thought it possible that he had not been sleeping very well. In this surmise he was right.

'About Margot—' began the young man. Mr Machfield smiled. He had met Margot, had entertained the young people to dinner at his flat, and twice had invited them to a theatre party.

Kenneth took a letter from his pocket and passed it across to his friend, and Machfield opened and read it.

Dear Kenneth: I'm not seeing you any more. I'm broken hearted to tell you this. Please don't try to see me—please! M.

'When did this come?'

'Last night. Naturally, I went to her flat. She was out. I went to her office—she was out. I was late for the bank and got it hot and strong from the manager. To make matters worse, there's a fellow dunning me for two hundred pounds—everything comes at once. I borrowed the money from father. What with one thing and another I'm desperate.'

Mr Machfield rose from his chair.

'Come home and have a meal, he said. 'As for the money—'

'No, no, no!' Kenneth McKay was panic-stricken. 'I don't want to borrow from you.' For a moment he sat in silence, then: 'Do you know a man named Reeder—J.G. Reeder?'

Machfield shook his head.

'He's a detective,' explained Kenneth. 'He has a big bank practice. He was down at our place today—weird-looking devil. If he could be a detective anybody could be!'

Mr Machfield said he recalled the name.

'He was in that railway robbery, wasn't he? J.G. Reeder—yes. Pretty smart fellow—young?'

'He's as old as—well, he's pretty old. And rather old-fashioned.'

Rufus snapped his finger to the waiter and paid his bill.

'You'll have to take pot luck—but Lamontaine is a wonderful cook. He didn't know that he was until I made him try.'

So they went together to the little flat in Park Lane. and Lamontaine, the pallid, middle-aged valet who spoke English with no trace of a foreign accent, prepared a meal that justified the praise of his master. In the middle of the dinner the subject of Mr Reeder arose again.

'What brought him to Beaconsfield—is there anything wrong at your bank?'

Rufus saw the young man's face go red.

'Well—there has been money missing; not very large sums. I have my own opinion, but it isn't fair to—well, you know.'

He was rather incoherent, and Mr Machfield did not pursue the inquiry.

'I hate the bank anyway—I mean the work. But I had to do something, and when I left Uppingham my father put me there—in the bank, I mean. Poor chap, he lost his money at Monte Carlo or somewhere—enormous sums. You wouldn't dream that he was a gambler. I'm not complaining, but it's a little trying sometimes.'

Mr Machfield accompanied him to the door that night and shivered.

'Cold—shouldn't be surprised if we had snow,' he said.

In point of fact the snow did not come until a week later. It started as rain and became snow in the night, and in the morning people who lived in the country looked out upon a white world: trees that bore a new beauty and hedges that showed their heads above sloping drifts.

II. — MURDER!

THERE was a car coming from the direction of Beaconsfield. The man on the motorcycle in the centre of the snowy road watched the lights grow brighter and brighter. Presently, in the glare of the headlamps, the driver of the car saw the motor cyclist, realized it was a policeman, saw the lift of his gloved hand and stopped the car. It was not difficult to stop, for the wheels were racing on the surface of the road, which had frozen into the worst qualities of ice. And snow was falling on top of this.

'Anything wrong—'

The driver began to shout the question, and then saw the huddled figure on the ground. It lay limply like a fallen sack; seemed at first glimpse to have nothing of human shape or substance.

The driver jumped out and went ploughing through the frozen snow.

'I just spotted him when I saw you,' said the policeman. 'Do you mind turning your car just a little to the right—I want more light on him.'

He dismounted, propped up his bike and went heavy-footed to where the man lay.

The second inmate of the car got to the wheel and turned the vehicle with some difficulty so that the light blazed on the dreadful thing.

Then he got out of the car, lingered nervously by the motor bike and finally joined the other two.

'It's old Wentford,' said the policeman.

'Wentford... good God!'

The first of the two motorists fell on his knees by the side of the body and peered down into the grinning face.

Old Benny Wentford!

'Good God!' he said again.

He was a middle-aged lawyer, unused to such a horror. Nothing more terrible had disturbed the smooth flow of his life than an occasional quarrel with the secretary of his golf club. Now here was death, violent and hideous—a dead man on a snowy road... a man who had telephoned to him two hours before, begging him to leave a party and come to him, though the snow had begun to fall all over again.

'You know Mr Wentford—he has told me about you.'

'Yes, I know him. I've often called at his house—in fact, I called there tonight but it was shut up. He made arrangements with the Chief Constable that I should call... h'm!'

The policeman stood over the body, his hands on his hips.

'You stay here—I'll go and phone the station,' he said.

He got on the motorbike and kicked it to life.

'Er... don't you think we'd better go?' Mr Enward, the lawyer, asked nervously. He had no desire to be left alone in the night with a battered corpse and a clerk whose trembling was almost audible.

'You couldn't turn your car,' said the policeman—which was true, for the lane was very narrow.

They heard the sound of the engine and presently they heard it no more.

'Is he dead, Mr Enward?' The young man's voice was hollow.

'Yes... I think so... the policeman said so.'

'Oughtn't we to make sure? He may only be... injured?'

Mr Enward had seen the face in the shadow of an uplifted shoulder. He did not wish to see it again.

'Better leave him alone till a doctor comes... it is no use interfering in these things. Wentford... good God!'

'He's always been a little bit eccentric, hasn't he?' The clerk was young and, curiosity being the tonic of youth, he had recovered some of his courage. 'Living alone in that tiny cottage with all his money. I was cycling past it on Sunday—a concrete box: that's what my girl friend called it. With all his money—'

'He is dead, Henry,' said Mr Enward severely, 'and a dead person has no property. I don't think it quite—um—seemly to talk of him in—um—his presence.'

He felt the occasion called for an emotional display of some kind. He had never grown emotional over clients; least of all could this tetchy old man inspire such feeling. A few words of prayer perhaps would not be out of place. But Mr Enward was a churchwarden of a highly respectable church and for forty years had had his praying done for him. If he had been a dissenter... but he was not. He wished he had a prayer book.

'He's a long time gone.'

The policeman could not have got far, but it seemed a very long time since he had left.

'Has he any heirs?' asked the clerk professionally.

Mr Enward did not answer. Instead, he suggested that the lights of the car should be dimmed. They revealed this Thing too plainly. Henry went back and the lights. It became terribly dark when the lights were lowered, and eyesight played curious tricks: it seemed that the bundle moved. Mr Enward had a feeling that the grinning face was lifting to leer slyly at him over the humped shoulder.

'Put on the lights again, Henry,' the lawyer's voice quavered. 'I can't see what I am doing.'

He was doing nothing; on the other hand, he had a creepy feeling that the Thing was behaving oddly. Yet it lay very still, just as it had lain all the time.

'He must have been murdered. I wonder where they went to?' asked H hollowly, and a cold shiver vibrated down Mr Enward's spine.

Murdered! Of course he was murdered. There was blood on the snow, and the murderers were...

He glanced backward nervously and almost screamed. A man stood in the shadowy space behind the car: the car lights reflected by the snow just revealed him.

'Who... who are you, please?' croaked the lawyer.

He added 'please' because there was no sense in being rough with a man who might be a murderer.

The figure moved into the light. He was slightly bent and even more middle-aged than Mr Enward. He wore a strange black hat, a long raincoat and large, shapeless gloves. About his neck was an enormous yellow scarf, and Mr Enward noticed, in a numb, mechanical way, that his shoes were large and square toed and that he carried a tightly furled umbrella on his arm though the snow was falling heavily.

'I'm afraid my car has broken down a mile up the road.' His voice was gentle and apologetic; obviously he had not seen the bundle. In his agitation Mr Enward had stepped into the light of the lamps and his black shadow sprawled across the deeper shadow.

'Am I wrong in thinking that you are in the same predicament?' asked the newcomer. 'I was unprepared for the—er—condition of the road. It is lamentable that one should have overlooked this possibility.'

'Did you pass the policeman?' asked Mr Enward. Whoever this stranger was, whatever might be his character and disposition, it was right and fair that he should know there was a policeman in the vicinity.

'Policeman?' The man was surprised. 'No, I passed no policeman. At my rate of progress it was very difficult to pass anything—'

'Going towards you... on a motorbike,' said Mr Enward rapidly. 'He said that he would be back soon. My name is Enward—solicitor—Enward, Caterham and Enward.'

He felt it was a moment for confidence.

'Delighted!' murmured the other. 'We've met before. My name—er—is Reeder—R, double E, D, E, R.'

Mr Enward took a step forward.

'Not the detective? I thought I'd seen you... look!' He stepped out of the light and the heap on the ground emerged from shadow. The lawyer made a dramatic gesture. Mr Reeder came forward slowly.

He stooped over the dead man, took a torch from his pocket and shone it steadily on the face. For a long time he looked and studied. His melancholy face showed no evidence that he was sickened or pained.

'H'm!' he said, and got up dusting the snow from his knee. He fumbled in the recesses of his overcoat, produced a pair of glasses, put them on awkwardly and surveyed the lawyer over their top.

'Very—um—extraordinary. I was on my way to see him.'

Enward stared.

'You were on your way? So was I! Did you know him?'

Mr Reeder considered this question.

'I—er—didn't—er—know him. No, I had never met him.'

The lawyer felt that his own presence needed some explanation.

'This is my clerk, Mr Henry Greene.'

Mr Reeder bowed slightly.

'What happened was this...'

He gave a very detailed and graphic description, which began with the recounting of what he had said when the telephone call came through to him at Beaconsfield, and how he was dressed and what his wife had said when she went to find his Wellington boots—her first husband had died through an ill-judged excursion into the night air on as foolish a journey—and how much trouble he had had starting the car, and how long he had had to wait for Henry.

Mr Reeder gave the impression that he was not listening. Once he walked out of the blinding light and peered back the way the policeman had gone; once he went over to the body and looked at it again; but most of the time he was wandering down the lane, searching the ground with his torch, with Mr Enward following at his heels lest any of his narrative be lost.

'Is he dead... I suppose so?' suggested the lawyer.

'I—er—have never seen anybody—er—deader,' said Mr Reeder gently. 'I should say, with all reverence and respect, that he was—er—extraordinarily dead.'

He looked at his watch.

'At nine-fifteen you met the policeman? He had just discovered the body? It is now nine thirty-five. How did you know that it was nine-fifteen?'

'I heard the church clock at Woburn Green strike the quarter.'

Mr Enward conveyed the impression that the clock struck exclusively for him. Henry halved the glory: he also had heard the clock.

'At Woburn Green—you heard the clock? H'm... nine-fifteen!'

The snow was falling thickly now. It fell on the heap and lay in the little folds and creases of his clothes. 'He must have lived somewhere about here?' Mr Reeder asked the question with great deference.

'My directions were that his house lay off the main road you would hardly call this a main road... fifty yards beyond a noticeboard advertising land for sale—desirable building land.'

Mr Enward pointed to the darkness.

'Just there—the noticeboard. Curiously enough, I am the—er—solicitor for the vendor,'

His natural inclination was to emphasize the desirability of the land, but he thought it was hardly the moment. He returned to the question of Mr Wentford's house.

'I've only been inside the place once—two years ago, wasn't it, Henry?'

'A year and nine months,' said Henry exactly. His feet were cold, his spine chilled. He felt sick.

'You cannot see it from the lane,' Enward continued. 'Rather a small, one- storey cottage. He had it specially built for him apparently. It isn't exactly... a palace.'

'Dear me!' said Mr Reeder, as though this were the most striking news he had heard that evening. 'In a house he built himself! I suppose he has, or had, a telephone?'

'He telephoned to me,' said Mr Enward; 'therefore he must have a telephone.'

Mr Reeder frowned as though he were trying to pick holes in the logic of this statement.

'I'll go along and see if it is possible to get through to the police,' he suggested.

'The police have already been notified,' said the lawyer hastily. 'I think we all ought to stay here together till somebody arrives.'

The man in the black hat, now absurdly covered with snow, shook his head. He pointed.

'Woburn Green is there. Why not go and arouse the—um—local constabulary?'

That idea had not occurred to the lawyer. His instinct urged him to return the way he had come and regain touch with realities in his own prosaic parlour.

'But do you think...' he blinked down at the body. 'I mean, it's hardly an act of humanity to leave him—'

'He feels nothing. He is probably in heaven,' said Mr Reeder, and added. 'Probably. Anyway, the police will know exactly where they can find him.'

There was a sudden screech from Henry. He was holding out his hand in the light of the torch.

'Look—blood!' he screamed.

There was blood on his hand, certainly.

'Blood—I didn't touch him! You know that, Mr Enward—I ain't been near him!'

Alas for our excellent educational system; Henry was reverting. 'Not near him I ain't been— blood!'

'Don't squeak, please.' Mr Reeder was firm. 'What have you touched?'

'Nothing—I only touched myself.'

'Then you have touched nothing,' said Mr Reeder with unusual acidity. 'Let me look.'

The rays of his torch travelled over the shivering clerk.

'It is on your sleeve—h'm!'

Mr Enward stared. There was a red, moist patch of some thing on Henry's sleeve.

'You had better go on to the police station,' said Mr Reeder. 'I'll come and see you in the morning.'

III. — THE RED ACES

ENWARD sat himself gratefully in the driver's seat, keeping some distance between himself and his shivering clerk. The car was on a declivity and would start without trouble. He turned the wheels straight and took off the brake. The vehicle skidded and slithered forward, and presently Mr Reeder, following in its wake, heard the sound of the running engine.

His torch showed him the noticeboard in the field, and fifty yards beyond he came to a path so narrow that two men could not walk abreast. It ran off from the road at right angles, and up this he turned, progressing with great difficulty, for he had heavy nails in his shoes. At last he saw a small garden gate on his right, set between two unkempt hedges. The gate was open, and this methodical man stopped to examine it by the light of his torch.

He expected to find blood and found it; just a smear. No marks on the ground, but then the snow would have obliterated those. It had not obliterated the print of footmarks going up the winding path. They were rather small, and he thought they were recently made. He kept his light on them until they led him into view of the squat house with its narrow windows and doorways. As he turned he saw a light gleam between curtains. He had a feeling that somebody was looking out at him. In another moment the light had vanished. But there was somebody in the house.

The footsteps led up to the door. Here he paused and knocked. There was no answer, and he knocked again more loudly. The chill wind sent the snowflakes swirling about him. Mr Reeder, who had a secret sense of humour, smiled. In the remote days of his youth his favourite Christmas card was one which showed a sparkling Father Christmas knocking at the door of a wayside cottage. He pictured himself as a bowler-hatted Father Christmas, and the whimsical fancy slightly pleased him.

He knocked a third time and listened; then, when no answer came, he stepped back and walked to the room where he had seen the light and tried to peer between the curtains. He thought he heard a sound—a thud—but it was not in the house. It might have been the wind. He looked round and listened, but the thud was not repeated, and he returned to his ineffectual starings.

There was no sign of a fire. He came back to knock for the fourth time, then tried the other side of the building, and here he made a discovery. A narrow casement window, deeply recessed and made of iron, was swaying to and fro in the wind, and beneath the window was a double set of footmarks, one coming and one going. They went away in the direction of the lane.

He came back to the door, and stood debating with himself what steps he should take. He had seen in the darkness two small white squares at the top of the door, and had thought they were little panes of toughened glass such as one sees in the tops of such doors. But, probably in a gust of wind, one of them became detached and fell at his feet. He stooped and picked it up: it was a playing card—the ace of diamonds. He put his torch on the second: it was the ace of hearts. They had both apparently been fastened side by side to the door with pins—black pins. Perhaps the owner of the house had put them there. Possibly they had some significance, fulfilled the function of mascots.

No answer came to his knocking, and Mr Reeder heaved a deep sigh. He hated climbing; he hated more squeezing through narrow windows into unknown places; more especially as there was probably somebody inside who would treat him rudely. Or they might have gone. The footprints, he found, were fresh; they were scarcely obliterated, though the snow was falling heavily. Perhaps the house was empty, and its inmate, whose light he had seen, had got away while he was knocking at the door. He would not have heard him jump from the window, the snow was too soft. Unless that thud he had heard—Mr Reeder gripped the sill and drew himself up, breathing heavily, though he was a man of considerable strength.

There were only two ways to go into the house: one was feet first, the other head first. He made a reconnaissance with his torch and saw that beneath the window was a small table, standing in a tiny room which had evidently been used as a cloakroom, for there were a number of coats hanging on hooks. It was safe to go in head first, so he wriggled down on to the table, feeling extraordinarily undignified.

He was on his feet in a moment, gripped the handle of the door gingerly and opened it. He was in a small hall, from which one door opened. He tried this: it was fast, and yet not fast. It was as though somebody was leaning against it on the other side. A quick jerk of his shoulder, and it flew open. Somebody tried to dash past him, but Mr Reeder was expecting that and worse. He gripped the fugitive.

'I'm extremely sorry,' he said in his gentle voice. 'It is a lady, isn't it?'

He heard her heavy breathing, a sob...

'Is there a light?'

He groped inside the lintel of the door, found a switch and turned it. Nothing happened for a moment, and then the lights came on suddenly. There was apparently a small generator at the back of the house which operated when any switch was turned on.

'Come in here, will you, please?'

He pressed her very gently into the room. Pretty, extraordinarily pretty. He did not remember ever having met a young lady who was quite as pretty as this particular young lady, though she was very white and her hair was in disorder, and on her feet were snow-boots the impression of which he had already seen in the snow.

'Will you sit down, please?'

He closed the door behind him.

'There's nothing to be afraid of. My name is Reeder.'

She had been terrified for that moment; now she looked up at him intensely.

'You're the detective?' she shivered. 'I'm so frightened. I'm so frightened!'

Mr Reeder looked round the room. It was pleasantly furnished—not luxuriously so but pleasantly. Evidently a sitting-room. Except that the mantelpiece had fallen or had been dragged on the floor, there was no sign of disorder. The hearth was littered with broken china ornaments and vases; the board itself was still held in position at one end. The fireplace and the blue hearthrug were curiously stained. And there were other little splodges of darkness on the surface of the carpet, and a flowerpot was knocked down near the door.

He saw a wastepaper basket and turned over its contents. Covers of little books apparently— there were five of them, but no contents. By the side of the fireplace was a dwarf bookcase. The books were dummies. He pulled one end of the case and it swung out, being hinged at the other end.

'H'm!' said Mr Reeder, and pushed the shelves back into their original position.

There was a cap on the floor by the table and he picked it up. It was wet. He examined it, thrust it into his pocket and turned his attention to the girl.

'How long have you been here, Miss—I think you'd better tell me your name.'

She was looking up at him.

'Half an hour. I don't know... it may be longer.'

'Miss—?' he asked again.

'Lynn—Margot Lynn.'

He pursed his lips thoughtfully.

'Margot Lynn. And you've been here half an hour. Who else has been here?'

'Nobody,' she said, springing to her feet. 'What has happened? Did he—did they fight?'

He put his hand on her shoulder gently and pressed her down into the chair.

'Did who fight whom?' asked Mr Reeder. His English was always very good on these occasions.

'Nobody has been here,' she said inconsequently.

Mr Reeder passed the question. 'You came from—?'

'I came from Bourne End station. I walked here. I often come that way. I'm Mr Wentford's secretary.'

'You walked here at nine o'clock because you're Mr Wentford's secretary? That was a very odd thing to do.'

She was searching his face fearfully. 'Has anything happened? Are you from the police? Has anything happened to Mr Wentford? Tell me, tell me!'

'He was expecting me: you knew that?'

She nodded. Her breath was coming quickly. He thought she found breathing a painful process.

'He told me—yes. I didn't know what it was about. He wanted his lawyer here too. I think he was in some kind of trouble.'

'When did you see him last?'

She hesitated. 'I spoke to him on the telephone—once, from London. I haven't seen him for two days.'

'And the person who was here?' asked Mr Reeder after a pause.

'There was nobody here! I swear there was nobody here!' She was frantic in her desire to convince him. 'I've been here half an hour—waiting for him. I let myself in—I have a key. There it is.'

She fumbled with trembling hands in her bag and produced a ring with two keys, one larger than the other.

'He wasn't here when I came in. I—I think he must have gone to London. He is very—peculiar.'

Mr J.G. Reeder put his hand in his pocket, took out two playing cards and laid them on the table.

'Why did he have those pinned to his door?'

She looked at him round-eyed.

'Pinned to his door?'

'The outer door,' said Mr Reeder, 'or, as he would call it, the street door.'

She shook her head.

'I've never seen them before. He's not the kind of man to put up things like that. He is very retiring and hates drawing attention to himself.'

'He was very retiring,' repeated Mr Reeder, 'and hated drawing attention to himself.'

IV. — J.G. REEDER'S THEORY

SOMETHING in his tone emphasized the tense he used. She shrank back.

'Was?' Her voice was a whisper. 'He's not dead... oh, my God! he's not dead?'

Mr Reeder smoothed his chin.

'Yes, I'm afraid—um—he is dead.'

She clutched the edge of the table for support. Mr Reeder had never seen such horror, such despair in a human face before,

'Was it... an accident—or—or—'

'You're trying to say "murder",' said Reeder gently. 'Yes, I'm very much afraid it was murder.'

He caught her in his arms as she fell and, laying her on the sofa, went in search of water. The taps were frozen, but he found some water in a kettle and, filling a glass with this, he returned to sprinkle it on her face, having a vague idea that something of the sort was necessary; but he found her sitting up, her face in her hands.

'Lie down, my dear, and keep quiet,' said Mr Reeder, and she obeyed meekly.

He looked round the room. The thing that struck him anew was the revolver which hung on the wall near the right-hand side of the fireplace just above the bookcase. It was placed to the hand of anybody who sat with his back to the window. Behind the armchair was a screen, and, tapping it, Mr Reeder discovered that it was of sheet iron.

He went outside to look at the door, turning on the hall light. It was a very thick door, and the inside was made of quarter-inch steel plate, screwed firmly to the wood. Leading from the kitchen was the bedroom, evidently Wentford's. The only light here was admitted from an oblong window near the ceiling. There was no other window, and about the narrow window was a stout steel cage. On the wall by the bed hung a second gun. He found a third weapon in the kitchen and behind a coat hanging in the hall, a fourth.

The cottage was a square box of concrete. The roof, as he afterwards learned, was tiled of sheet iron, and, except for the window through which he had squeezed, there was none by which ingress could be had.

He was puzzled why this man, who evidently feared attack, had left any window so large as that through which he had come. He afterwards found the broken wire which must have set an alarm bell ringing when the window was opened.

There was blood on the mat in the hall, blood in the tiny lobby. He came back to where the girl was lying and sniffed. There was no smell of cordite, and having seen the body, he was not surprised.

'Now my dear.'

She sat up again.

'I am not a police officer; I am a—er—a gentleman called in by your friend, Mr Wentford—your late friend,' he corrected himself, 'to do something—I know not what! He called me by phone; I gave him my—um—terms, but he offered me no reason why he was sending for me. You, as his secretary, may perhaps—'

She shook her head.

'I don't know. He'd never mentioned you before he spoke to me on the telephone.'

'I'm not a policeman,' said Mr Reeder again, and his voice was very gentle; 'therefore, my dear, you need have few qualms about telling me the truth, because these gentlemen, when they come, these very active and intelligent men, will probably discover all that I have seen, even if I did not tell them. Who was the man who went out of this house when I knocked at the door?'

Her face was deathly pale, but she did not flinch. He wondered if she was as pretty when she was not so pale. Mr Reeder wondered all sorts of odd little things like that; his mind could never stagnate.

'There was nobody—in this house—since I have been here—'

Mr Reeder did not press her. He sighed, closed his eyes, shook his head, shrugged his shoulders. 'It's a great pity,' he said. 'Can you tell me anything about Mr Wentford?'

'No,' she said in a low voice. 'He was my uncle. I think you ought to know that. He didn't want anybody to know, but that must come out. He's been very good to us—he sent my mother abroad; she's an invalid. I conducted his business.' All this very jerkily.

'Have you been here often?'

She shook her head.

'Not often,' she said. 'We usually met somewhere by appointment, generally in a lonely place where one wouldn't be likely to meet anybody who knew us. He was very shy of strangers, and he didn't like anybody coming here.'

'Did he ever entertain friends here?'

'No.' She was very emphatic. 'I'm sure he didn't. The only person he ever saw was the police patrol on this beat. Uncle used to make him coffee every night. I think it was for the company— he told me he felt lonely at nights. The policeman kept an eye on him. There are two—Constable Steele and Constable Verity. My uncle always sent them a turkey at Christmas. Whoever was on duty used to come up here on his motorbike.'

The telephone was in the bedroom and Mr Reeder remembered he had promised to phone. He got through to a police station and asked a few questions. When he got back he found the girl by the window, looking between the curtains.

Somebody was coming up the path. They could hear voices and, looking through the curtain, he saw a string of torches and went out to meet a local sergeant and two men. Behind them was Mr Enward. Reeder wondered what had become of Henry. Possibly he had been lost in the snow; the thought interested him.

'This is Mr Reeder.' Enward's voice was shrill. 'Did you telephone?'

'Yes, I telephoned. We have a young lady here—Mr Wentford's niece.'

Enward repeated the words, surprised. 'His niece here? Really? I knew he had a niece. In fact—' He coughed. It was an indelicate moment to speak of legacies.

'She'll be able to throw some light on this business,' said the sergeant, more practical and less delicate.

'She could throw no light on any business,' said Mr Reeder, very firmly for him. 'She was not here when the crime was committed—in fact, she arrived some time after. She has a key which admitted her. Miss Lynn acts as her uncle's secretary, all of which facts, gentlemen, I think you should know.'

The sergeant was not quite sure about the propriety of noticing Mr Reeder. To him he was almost a civilian, a man without authority, and his presence was therefore irregular. Nevertheless, some distant echo of J.G. Reeder's fame had penetrated into Buckinghamshire. The police officer seemed to remember that Mr Reeder either occupied or was about to occupy a semi- official position remotely associated with police affairs. If he had been a little clearer on the subject he would also have been more definite in his attitude. Since he was not so sure, it was expedient, until Mr Reeder's position became established, to ignore his presence—a peculiarly difficult course to follow when an officially absent person is standing at your elbow, murmuring flat contradictions of your vital theories.

'Perhaps you'll tell me why you are here, sir?' said the sergeant with a certain truculence.

Mr Reeder felt in his pocket, took out a large leather case and laid it carefully on the table, first dusting the table with the side of his hand; then he unfolded the case and took out, with exasperating deliberation, a thick pad of telegrams. He fixed his glasses and examined the telegrams one by one, reading each through. At last he shook one clear and handed it to the officer. It ran:

'WISH TO CONSULT WITH YOU TONIGHT ON VERY IMPORTANT MATTER. CALL ME WOBURN GREEN 971. VERY URGENT. WENTFORD.'

'You're a private detective, Mr Reeder?'

'More intimate than private,' murmured that gentleman. 'In these days of publicity one has little more than the privacy of a goldfish in his crystal habitation.'

The sergeant saw something in the wastepaper basket and pulled it out. It was a small loose-leafed book. There was another, indeed, many. He piled five on the table; but they were merely the covers and nothing more.

'Diaries,' said Mr Reeder gently. 'You will observe that each one is dingier than the other.'

'But how do you know they're diaries?' demanded the police officer testily.

'Because the word "diary" is printed on the inside covers,' said Mr Reeder, more gently than ever.

This proved to be the case, though the printing had been overlooked. Mr Reeder had not overlooked it; he had not even overlooked the two scraps of burnt paper on the hearth, all that remained of those diaries.

'There is a safe let into the wall behind that bookcase.' He pointed. 'It may or may not be full of clues. I should imagine it is not. But I shouldn't touch it if I were you, Sergeant,' he said hastily, 'not without gloves. Those detestable fellows from Scotland Yard will be here eventually, and they'll be very rude if they photograph a fingerprint and find it's yours.'

Gaylor of the Yard came at half past two. He had been brought out of his bed through a blinding snowstorm and along a road that was thoroughly vile.

The girl had gone home. Mr Reeder was sitting meditatively before the fire which he had made up, smoking the cheapest kind of cigarette.

'Is the body here?'

Mr Reeder shook his head.

'Have they found that motor cycle policeman, Verity?'

Again Mr Reeder signalled a negative. 'They found his bike on the Beaconsfield road with bloodstains on the saddle.'

He was staring into the fire, the cigarette drooping limply from his mouth, on his face an air of unsettled melancholy; he did not even turn his head to address Inspector Gaylor.

'The young lady has gone home, as I said. The local constabulary gave you particulars of the lady, of course. She acted as secretary to the late Mr Wentford, and he appears to have been very fond of her, since he has left his fortune two-thirds to the young lady and one-third to his sister. There is no money in the house as far as can be ascertained, but he banks with the Great Central Bank, Beaconsfield branch.' Reeder fumbled in his pocket. 'Here are the two aces.'

'The two what?' asked the puzzled inspector.

'The two aces.' Mr Reeder passed the playing cards over his shoulder, his eyes still on the fire. 'The ace of diamonds, and I believe the ace of hearts—I am not very well acquainted with either.'

'Where did you get these?'

The other explained, and Gaylor examined the aces.

'Why are you so sure that these cards were put up after the murder — why shouldn't they have been put up before?'

J.G. groaned at his scepticism and, reaching out, took a pack of cards from a little table.

'You will find the two aces missing from this pack. You would have also found that two cards had been stuck together. Blood does that. No fingerprints. I should imagine the cards were sorted over after the untimely demise of Mr Wentford, and the two significant aces extracted and exhibited.'

The inspector made a very careful search of the bedroom and came back to find Mr Reeder nodding himself to sleep.

'What did they do to the girl—these local blokes?' asked Gaylor coarsely.

Reeder's right shoulder came up in a lazy shrug.

'They escorted her to the station and took a statement from her. The inspector was kind enough to furnish me with a copy—you'll find it on this table. They also examined her hands and her clothes, but it was quite unnecessary. There is corroborative evidence that she arrived at Bourne End station at twelve minutes past eight as she says she did—the murder was committed at forty minutes past seven, a few minutes before or after.'

'How on earth do you know that? Is there any proof?'

Mr Reeder shook his head. 'A romantic surmise.' He sighed heavily. 'You have to realize, my dear Gaylor, that I have a criminal mind. I see the worst in people and the worst in every human action. It is very tragic. There are moments when—' He sighed again. 'Forty minutes past seven,' he said simply. 'That is my romantic surmise. The doctor will probably confirm my view. The body lay here,' he pointed to the hearthrug, 'until—well, quite a considerable time.'

Gaylor was skimming two closely written sheets of foolscap. Suddenly he stopped.

'You're wrong,' he said. 'Listen to this statement made at the station by Miss Lynn. "I rang up my uncle from the station, telling him I might be late because of the snowy road. He answered 'Come as soon as you can.' He spoke in a very low tone; I thought he sounded agitated!" That knocks your theory about the time a bit skew-whiff, eh?'

Mr Reeder looked round and blinked open his eyes.

'Yes, doesn't it? It must have been terribly embarrassing.'

'What was embarrassing?' asked the puzzled police officer.

'Everything,' mumbled Mr Reeder, his chin falling on his chest.

V. — THE MISSING POLICEMAN

'THE trouble about Reeder,' said Gaylor to the superintendent in the course of a long telephone conversation, 'is that you feel he does know something which he shouldn't know. I've never seen him in a case where he hasn't given me the impression that he was the guilty party—he knew so much about the crime.'

'Humour him,' said the superintendent. 'He'll be in the Public Prosecutor's Department one of these days. He never was in a case that he didn't make himself an accessory by pinching half the clues.'

At five o'clock the detective shook the sleeper awake.

'You'd better go home, old man,' he said. 'We'll leave an officer in charge here.'

Mr Reeder rose with a groan, splashed some soda-water from a syphon into a glass and drank it.

'I must stay, I'm afraid, unless you've any very great objection.'

'What's the idea of waiting?' asked Gaylor in surprise.

Mr Reeder looked from side to side as though he were seeking an answer.

'I have a theory—an absurd one, of course—but I believe the murderers will come back. And honestly I don't think your policeman would be of much use, unless you were inclined to give the poor fellow the lethal weapon necessary to defend himself.'

Gaylor sat down squarely before him, his large gloved hands on his knees.

'Tell papa,' he said.

Mr Reeder looked at him pathetically.

'There is nothing to tell, my dear Mr Gaylor; merely suspicion, bred, as I said, in my peculiarly morbid mind, having perhaps no foundation in fact. Those two cards, for example—that was a stupid piece of bravado. But it has happened before. You remember the Teignmouth case, and the Lavender Hill case, with the man with the slashed chest?'

Gaylor took the cards from his pocket and examined them.

'A bit of tomfoolery,' was his verdict.

Mr Reeder sighed and shook his head at the fire.

'Murderers as a rule have no sense of humour. They are excitable people, frightened people, but they are never comic people.'

He walked to the door and pulled it open. Snow had ceased to fall. He came back.

'Where is the policeman you propose leaving on duty?' he asked.

'I'll find one,' said Gaylor. 'There are half a dozen within call. A whistle will bring one along.'

Mr Reeder looked at him thoughtfully.

'I don't think I should. Let's wait until daylight—or perhaps you wish to go? I don't think anybody would harm you. I rather fancy they would be glad to see the back of you.'

'Harm me?' said Gaylor indignantly, but Reeder took no notice of the interruption.

'My own idea is that I should brew a dish of tea, and possibly fry a few eggs. I'm rather hungry.'

Gaylor walked to the door and frowned out into the darkness. He had worked with Reeder before, and was too wise a man to reject the advice summarily. Besides, if Reeder was entering or had entered the Public Prosecutor's Department, he would occupy a rank equivalent to superintendent.

'I'm all for eggs,' said Gaylor, and bolted the outer door.

The older man disappeared into the kitchen and came back with a kettle, which he placed on the fire, went out again and returned with a frying- pan.

'Do you ever take your hat off?' asked Gaylor curiously.

Mr Reeder did not turn his head, but shook the pan gently to ensure an even distribution of the boiling fat.

'Very rarely,' he said. 'On Christmas Days sometimes.'

And then Gaylor asked a fatuous question; at least, it sounded fatuous to him, and yet subconsciously he felt that the other might supply an immediate answer.

'Who killed Wentford?'

'Two men, possibly three,' said Mr Reeder instantly; 'but I rather think two. Neither was a professional burglar. One at any rate thought more of the killing than of any profit he might have got out of it. Neither found anything worth taking, and even if they had opened the safe they would have discovered nothing of value. The young lady, Miss Margot Lynn, could, I think, have saved them a lot of trouble in their search for treasure—I may be mistaken here, but I rarely fall into error. Miss Margot is—'

He stopped, looked round quickly.

'What is it?' asked Gaylor, but Reeder put his finger to his lips.

He rose, moving across the room to the door which led to the tiny lobby through which he had made his entrance. He stood with one hand on the knob, and Gaylor saw that in the other was a Browning. Slowly he turned the handle. The door was locked from the inside.

In two strides Reeder was at the front door, turned the key and pulled it open. Then, to the inspector's amazement, he saw his companion take one step and fall sprawling on his face in the snow. He ran to his assistance. Something caught him by the ankle and flung him forward.

Reeder was on his feet and assisted the other to rise.

'A little wire fastened between the door posts,' he explained. A bright beam shot out from his torch as he turned the corner of the house. There was nobody in sight, but the window, which he had fastened, was open and there were new footprints in the snow leading away into the darkness.

'Well, I'm damned!' said Gaylor.

J.G. Reeder said nothing. He was smiling when he came back into the room, having stopped to break the wire with a kick.

'Do you think somebody was in the lobby?'

'I know somebody was in the lobby,' he said. 'Dear me! How foolish of us not to have had a policeman posted outside the door! You notice that a pane of glass has been cut? Our friend must have been listening there.'

'Was there only one?'

'Only one,' said Mr Reeder gravely. 'But was he the one who came that way before—I don't think so.'

He took the frying-pan from the hearth where he had put it and resumed his frying of eggs, served them on two plates and brewed the tea. It was just as though death had not lurked in that lobby a few minutes before.

'No, they won't come back; there is no longer a reason for our staying. There were two, but only one came into the house. They may have a long way to travel, and they would not risk being anywhere near at daybreak. At six o'clock the agricultural labourer of whom the poet Gray wrote so charmingly will be on his way to work, and they won't risk meeting him either.'

They had a solemn breakfast, Gaylor plying the other with questions, which in the main he did not answer.

'You think that Miss Lynn is in this—in the murder, I mean?'

Reeder shook his head.

'No, no,' he said. 'I'm afraid it isn't as easy as that.'

Daylight had come greyly when, having installed a cold policeman in the house, they plodded down the lane. Reeder's car had been retrieved in the night, and a more powerful vehicle, fitted with wheel chains, was waiting to take them to Beaconsfield. They did not reach that place for two hours, for on their way they came upon a little knot of policemen and farm labourers looking sombrely at the body of Constable Verity. He lay under some bushes a few yards from the road, and he was dead.

'Shot,' said a police officer. 'The divisional surgeon has just seen him.'

Stiff and cold, with his booted legs stretched wide, his overcoat turned up and his snow-covered cap drawn over his eyes, was the officer who had ridden out from the station courtyard so unsuspectingly the night before. His bike had already been found; the bloodstains that had puzzled and alarmed the police were now accounted for.

Gaylor and Reeder drove on into Beaconsfield. Gaylor was a depressed and silent man; Mr Reeder was silent but not depressed.

As they came out into the main road he turned to his companion, and asked:

'I wonder why they didn't bring their own aces?'

VI. — THE VEILED WOMAN

MR KINGFETHER, manager of the Beaconsfield branch of the Great Central Bank, was at work very early that morning, for he had a letter to write, and his managerial office gave him the privacy he required. He was a serious man, with serious-looking glasses on a pale, plump face. He had a little black moustache and his cheeks and chin were invariably blue, for he had what barbers call a 'strong beard.'

The newspapers arrived as he was writing. They were pushed under the closed outer door of the bank and, being at the moment stuck for the alternative to an often reiterated term of endearment, he rose and brought them into the office and sat down to glance through them. There were two papers, one financial and one human.

He read the latter first, and there was the murder in detail, though it had only occurred the night before. The discovery of the constable's body was not described, because it had not been discovered when the paper went to press.

He read and re-read, his mind in a whirl, and then he took the telephone and called Mr Enward.

'Good morning, Kingfether... Yes, yes, it's true... I was practically a witness—they've found the poor policeman dead... yes, murdered... yes, shot... I was the last person to speak to him. Dreadful, dreadful, dreadful! That such horrors can be—I say that such horrors can be... I said that such... What's the matter with your phone? He banks with you? Really? Really? I'll come over and talk with you...'

Mr Kingfether hung up the telephone and wiped his face with his handkerchief. It was a face that became moist on the least provocation. Presently he folded the newspaper and looked at his unfinished letter. He was on the eighth page and the last words he had written were:

'... can hardly live the day through without seeing your darling face, my own...'

It was obvious that he was not writing to his general manager, or to a client who had overdrawn his account.

He added 'beloved' mechanically, though he had used the word a dozen times before. Then he unfolded the paper and read of the murder again.

A knock at the side door: he went out to admit Enward. The lawyer was more important than usual. Participation in public affairs has this effect. And a news agency had telephoned to ask whether they could send a photographer, and Mr Enward, shivering at the telephone in his pyjamas, had said 'Yes' and had been photographed at his breakfast table at 7.30 am, poising a cup of tea and looking excessively grave. He would presently appear in one hundred and fifty newspapers above the caption 'Lawyer Who Discovered His Own Client Murdered'.

'It's a terrible business,' said Enward, throwing off his coat. 'He banked with you? I'm in charge of his affairs, Kingfether, though heaven knows I'm ignorant about 'em! I don't know how he stands... what's his credit here?'

Mr Kingfether considered. 'I'll get the ledger from the safe,' he said.

He locked the centre drawer of his desk, because his letter to Ava Burslem was there and other documents, but Enward saw nothing offensive in the act of caution; rather was it commendable.

'Here's his account.' Kingfether laid the big ledger on the desk and opened it where his thumb marked a page. 'Credit three thousand four hundred pounds.'

Enward fixed his glasses and looked.

'Has he anything on deposit? Securities—no? Did he come often to the bank?'

'Never,' said Kingfether. 'He used the account to pay bills. When he wanted ready money he posted a bearer cheque and I posted back the money. He has, of course, sent people here to cash cheques.'

'That six hundred pounds withdrawn five days ago.' Enward pointed to the item.

'It's strange that you should point that out—it was paid over the counter four days ago. I didn't see the person who called for it—I was out. My clerk McKay cashed the cheque. Who's that?'

There was a gentle rapping at the door. Mr Kingfether went out of the room and came back with the caller.

'How fortunate to find you here!' said J.G. Reeder. He was spruce and lively. A barber had shaved him, somebody had cleaned his shoes. 'The account of the late Mr Wentford?' He nodded to the book.

It was generally known that J.G. Reeder acted for the Great Central Bank, and the manager did not question his title to ask questions. Mr Enward was not so sure.

'This is rather a serious matter, Mr Reeder,' he said, consciously grave. 'I am not so sure that we can take you into our confidence—'

'Hadn't you better see the police and ask them if they are prepared to take you into their confidence?' asked Mr Reeder, with a sudden ferocity which made the lawyer recoil.

Once more the manager explained the account.

'Six hundred pounds—h'm!' Mr Reeder frowned. 'A large sum—who was the drawer?'

'My clerk McKay said it was a lady—but she wore a thick veil.'

Reeder stared at him.

'Your clerk McKay? Of course—a fair young man. How stupid of me! Kenneth—or is it Karl—Kenneth, is it? H'm! A heavily veiled lady. Have you the number of the notes?'

Kingfether was taken aback by the question. He searched for a book that held the information, and Mr Reeder copied them down, an easy task since the tens and the fives ran consecutively.

'When does your clerk arrive?'

Kenneth was supposed to arrive at nine. As a rule he was late. He was late that morning.

Mr Reeder saw the young man through a window in the manager's office and thought that he did not look well. His eyes were tired; he had shaved himself carelessly, for his chin bore a strip of sticking plaster. Perhaps that accounted for the spots on the soiled cuff of his shirt, thought Mr Reeder, when he confronted the young man.

'No, I will see him alone,' said Reeder.

'He's rather an insolent pup,' warned Mr Kingfether.

'I have tamed lions,' said Mr Reeder.

When Kenneth came in:

'Close the door, please, and sit down. You know me, my boy?'

'Yes, sir,' said Kenneth.

'That is blood on your shirt cuff, isn't it?... cut your chin, did you? You haven't been home all night?'

Kenneth did not answer at once.

'No sir. I haven't changed my shirt, if that's what you mean.'

Mr Reeder smiled. 'Exactly.'

He fixed the young man with a long, searching glare. 'Why did you go to the house of the late Mr Wentford last night between the hours of eight- thirty and nine-thirty?'

He saw the youth go deathly white.

'I didn't know he was dead—I didn't even know his name until this morning. I went there because... well, I was low enough to spy on somebody... follow them from London and sneak into the house—'

'The young lady, Margot Lynn. You're in love with her? Engaged to her, perhaps?'

'I'm in love with her—I'm not engaged to her. We are no longer... friends,' said Kenneth in a low voice. 'She told you I'd been there, I suppose?' and then, as a light broke on him: 'Or did you find my cap? It had my name in it.'

Mr Reeder nodded. 'You came down on the same train as Miss Lynn? Good. Then you will be able to prove that you left Bourne End station—'

'No, I shan't,' said Kenneth. 'I slipped out of the train on to the line. Naturally I didn't want her to see me. I got out through the level crossing. There was nobody about—it was snowing heavily.'

'Very awkward.' Mr Reeder pursed his lips. 'You thought there was some sort of friendship between Mr Wentford and the young lady?'

Kenneth made a gesture of despair. 'I don't know what I thought—I was just a jealous fool.'

There was a long silence.

'You paid out six hundred pounds the other day to a lady on Mr Wentford's cheque?'

'I didn't know that Wentford was—' began Ken, but Mr Reeder brushed aside that aspect of the situation. 'Yes, a veiled lady. She came by car. It was a large sum of money, but the day before Mr Kingfether had told me to honour any cheque of Mr Wentford's no matter to whom the money was paid.'

J.G. Reeder asked very little more. He was, it seemed, the easiest man in the world to satisfy. Before he left he saw the manager alone.

'Did you tell Mr McKay that he was to honour any cheque of Mr Wentford's, no matter to whom the money was paid?'

The answer came instantly.

'Of course not! Naturally I should expect him to be sure that the person who presented a cheque had authority. And another curious thing which I have not mentioned. I lunch at the inn opposite and I usually have a seat in the window, where I can see these premises, but I have no recollection of any car drawing up to the bank.'

'H'm!' was all that Mr Reeder said.

He made a few inquiries in Beaconsfield and the neighbourhood and went on to Wentford's house, where Gaylor had arranged to meet him. The inspector was pacing up and down the snowy terrace in front of the house and he was in very good spirits.

'I think I've got the man,' he said. 'Do you know anybody named McKay?'

Mr Reeder looked at him slyly.

'I know a dozen,' he said.

'Come inside and I'll show you something.'

Reeder followed him into the room. The carpet had been taken up, the furniture moved. Evidently a very thorough search had been in progress. Gaylor swung back the bookcase: the safe door was ajar.

'We got the keys from the maker—quick work! They were down here by eight-thirty.'

He stooped down and pulled out three bundles. The first was made up of bills, the second of used cheques, the third was a thick bundle of French banknotes, each to the value of 1000 francs.

'That is surprise No. 1,' began the detective, flourishing the money. 'French money—'

'I'm afraid it doesn't surprise me,' said Mr Reeder apologetically. 'You see, I've been examining the gentleman's bank book. By the way, here are the numbers of notes drawn from Mr Wentford's account.' He handed over a slip of paper.

'Six hundred pounds is a lot of money,' said Gaylor. 'I'll phone these through. Well, what else did you find in the bank book?'

'I observed,' said Mr Reeder, 'though I will not emphasize the fact, that all the money he paid was in banknotes. Number 2 is—?'

The inspector extracted a sheet of headed paper from one heap. Written in pencil was what was evidently a memorandum from somebody who signed himself 'D. H. Hartford.'

'I have found that the man who is employing a detective to find you is George McKay of Sennet House, Marlow. I don't know what his intentions are, but they're not pleasant. There is nothing to worry about, he is employing one of the most incompetent private detectives in the business.'

'Extraordinary!' said Mr Reeder, and coughed.

'The first thing to do is to find Hartford—' began Gaylor.

'He's in Australia,' Mr Reeder interrupted. 'At the time that letter was written his office address was 327, Lambs Buildings. He became bankrupt and left the country hurriedly.'

'How do you know?' asked Gaylor, astonished.

'Because I—um—was the incompetent private detective engaged to find Mr Lynn or, as he called himself, Mr Wentford. And I didn't find him,' said Mr Reeder.

'Why did McKay want to find this man?'

'He owed him money. I know no more than that. The search fell off because—um—Mr McKay owed me money. One has to live.'

'Then you knew about Wentford?'

Mr Reeder took counsel with himself.

'Um—yes. I recognized him last night—I once had a photograph of him. I thought it was very odd. I also—er—drove over to Marlow and made inquiries. Mr McKay—Mr George McKay did not leave his house last night, and at the moment the murder was committed was entertaining the—um—vicar to dinner.'

'You're a killjoy,' Gaylor said, and Mr Reeder sighed heavily. Gaylor got up and stood squarely before him. 'What do you know about these murders, Reeder?' he challenged.

Mr Reeder spread his hands wide. His glasses, set askew, slipped a little further down his nose. He was not a very imposing figure.

'I am a strange man, Mr Gaylor; I am cursed, as you are aware, with a peculiarly evil mind. I am also intensely curious—I have always been. I am curious about criminals and chickens—I have perhaps the finest Rhode Island Reds in London, but that is by the way. It would be cruel to give you my theories. The blood on the policeman's motorcycle: that is interesting. And Henry—I suppose Mr Enward's clerk has another name—the blood on his coat, though he did not go near the body of the late Mr Wentford, that is interesting. Poor Henry is suffering from a severe chill and is in bed, but his mother, an admirable and hardworking woman, permitted me to see him. Then the two aces pinned to the door, all very, very, very interesting indeed! Mr Gaylor, if you will permit me to interview old George McKay I will undertake to tell you who committed these murders.'

'The girl told you something—the girl Lynn?'

'The girl has told me nothing. She also may be very informative. I propose spending a night or two in her flat—um—not, I hope, without a chaperone.'

Gaylor looked at him, amazed. Mr Reeder was blushing.

VII. — WHO KILLED WENTFORD?

THE last page of the letter which Eric Kingfether had begun with such ease in the early part of the morning was extremely difficult to compose. It had become necessary to say certain things; it was vital that he should not put his communication into writing.

In desperation he decided to make a break with practice. He would go to London. It was impossible to leave before the bank closed, but he could go immediately afterwards, though there was urgent work which should have kept him on the bank premises until six, and some private work of serious importance that should have occupied him until midnight. When the bank closed he handed over the key of the safe to Kenneth.

'I've been called to town. Balance up the books and put them in the safe. I'll be back by six; I'd like you to wait for me.'

Kenneth McKay did not receive the suggestion favourably. He also wished to get away.

'Well, you can't!' said the other sharply. 'The bank inspector will be in tomorrow to check the Wentford account. It will probably be required as evidence.'

Mr Kingfether got out his car and drove to London. He parked in a Bloomsbury square and made his way on foot to a big mansion block behind Gower Street. The elevator man who took him up grinned a welcome.

'The young lady's in, sir,' he said.

The 'young lady' herself opened the door to his ring. 'Look who's here!' she said in surprise, and stood aside to let him in.

She was wearing an old dressing gown and did not look as attractive as usual.

'In another half hour I'd have been out,' she said. 'I didn't get up till after lunch. These late nights are surely hell!'

She led the way to a sitting-room which was hazy with cigarette smoke. It was a large room, its floor covered with a soft carpet that had once cost a lot of money but was now mottled with stains. In front of the fire was a big divan, and on this she had been reclining. The furnishing and appointments of the room were of that style which is believed to be oriental by quite a large number of people. The whole room was half way to blowsiness. It had a stale, sweet scent.

'Well, my dear, what brings you up to town? I told you to snatch a few hours sleep—round about one you looked like a boiled owl, and that's not the state to be in when you're chasing money.'

She was dark and good-looking by certain standards. Her figure was robust, and nature had given generously to the amplification of her visible charms.

For a very long time they talked, head to head. She was an excellent listener; her sympathy had a sincere note. At half past five:

'Now off you pop and don't worry. The governor will be seeing you tonight—talk it over with him. I think you'd better, in case anything turns up... you know what I mean.'

He took a letter out of his pocket and gave it to her with an air of embarrassment.

'I wrote it, or rather started it, this morning... I couldn't finish it. I mean every word I say.'

She kissed him loudly.

'You're a darling!' she said.

Mr Kingfether came back to his office to find only a junior in charge. McKay, despite instructions to the contrary, had gone, and the manager sat down to a rough examination of important books in no condition to do justice to his task. He possessed one of those slow-starting tempers that gathers momentum from its own weight. A little grievance and a long brooding brought him to a condition of senseless and unrestrainable fury.

He was in this state when Kenneth McKay returned.

'I asked you to stay in, didn't I?' He glowered at his subordinate.

'Did you? Well, I stayed in until I finished my work. Then the bank inspector came.'

Mr Kingfether's face went white. 'What did he want? Redman didn't tell me he called.'

'Well, he did.' Kenneth passed into the outer office.

Kingfether sat scribbling oddly on his blotting-pad for a moment, and then for the first time saw the letter that had been placed on the mantelpiece. It was marked 'Urgent, confidential. Deliver by hand,' and was from head office.

He took it up with a shaking hand and, after a long hesitation, tore the seal. There was a small mirror on the wall above the fireplace, and he caught sight of his face and could hardly believe that that ghost of a man was himself.

There was no need to read the letter twice through. Already he knew every word, every comma. He stood blinking at his reflection, and then went into the outer office. He found Kenneth collecting some personal belongings from his desk.

'I suppose the inspector came about the Wentford cheque?' he said.

The young man looked round at him.

'Wentford cheque? I don't know what you're talking about. You don't mean the cheque I cashed for the woman?'

It required an effort on the manager's part to affirm this.

'What was wrong with it?'

'It was forged, that's all.'

'Forged?' Kenneth frowned at him.

'Yes... didn't the inspector say anything? He left a letter for me, didn't he?'

Kenneth shook his head.

'No. He was surprised to find that you weren't here. I told him you had gone up to head office. I'm getting a bit sick of lying about you. What's the yarn about this cheque?'

Again it required a painful effort on the manager's part to speak.

'It was forged. You've to report to head office tomorrow morning... some of the banknotes have been traced to you... the cheque was out of your office book.'

It was out, yet he felt no relief.

McKay was looking at him open-mouthed.

'You mean the cheque that was changed by that woman?'

The word 'woman' irritated Mr Kingfether.

'A lady was supposed to have called, a veiled lady—'

'What do you mean by "supposed"?' demanded Kenneth. 'You say that the notes were traced to me—I issued them: is that what you mean?'

'You have them—some of them—in your private possession;—that's all.'

Incredulity showed in Kenneth's face. 'Me? You mean that I stole them?'

Kingfether had reached the limit of endurance. 'How the hell do I know what you did?' he almost shouted. 'Head office have written to say that some of the notes you paid over the counter have been traced through a moneylender named Stuart to you.'

The young man's face changed suddenly.

'Stuart... Oh?' was all that he said. A moment later he went blundering out of the side door, leaving Mr Kingfether to continue his aimless scribblings on his blotting-pad.

Kenneth reached Marlow just before the dinner hour, and he came into the study where old George McKay was usually to be found, working out his eternal combinations. To Kenneth's amazement, his father greeted him with a smile. Instead of the cards, his table was covered with packages of documents and the paraphernalia of correspondence.

'Hullo, son—we've had a stroke of luck. The arbitrators have decided in my favour. I knew jolly well I hadn't parted with my rights to the dyeing process when I sold out, and the company has to pay close on a hundred thousand back royalties.'

Kenneth knew of this wrangle between his father and his late company that had gone on through the years, but he had never paid very much attention to it.

'That means a steady income for years, and this time I'm going to look after things—here!'

He pointed to the grate. The fireplace was filled with half-burnt playing cards.

'They've asked me to rejoin the board as chairman. What's the matter, Kenny?'

Kenneth was sitting on the opposite side of the table, and his father had seen his face.

Briefly he told his story, and George McKay listened without comment until he had finished.

'Wentford, eh? He's going to be a curse to me to the end of my days.'

Kenneth gasped his amazement. 'Did you know him?'

Old George nodded. 'I knew him all right!' he said grimly. 'Reeder was here this morning—'

'About me?' asked the other quickly.

'About me,' said his father. 'I rather gathered that he suspected me of the murder.'

Kenneth came to his feet, horrified. 'You? But he's mad! Why should you—'

Mr McKay smiled dourly. 'There was quite a good reason why I should murder him,' he said calmly; 'such a good reason that I have been expecting the police all the afternoon.'

Then abruptly he changed the subject.

'Tell me about these banknotes. Of course I knew that you had borrowed the money from Stuart, my boy. I was a selfish old man to let you do it—how did the money come to you?'

Kenneth's story was a surprising one. 'I had it a couple of days ago,' he said. 'I came flown to breakfast and found a letter. It wasn't registered and the address was hand printed, I opened it, without any idea of what it contained. Just then I was terribly upset about Stuart—I thought head office might get to know about my borrowing money. And when I found inside the letter twenty ten-pound notes you could have knocked me out.'

'Was there any letter?'

'None. Not even "from a friend."'

'Who knew about you being in debt?'

One name came instantly to Kenneth's mind.

'You told your Margot, did you... Wentford's niece? His real name was Lynn, by the way. Could she have sent it?'

'It wasn't her who drew the money, I'll swear! I should have known her. And though she wore a veil, I could recognize her again if I met her. Kingfether's line is that no woman came; he's suggesting that the cheque was cashed by me. He even says that the cheque was out of a book which I keep in my drawer for the use of customers who come to the bank without their cheque books.'

George McKay fingered his chin, his keen eyes on his son.

'If you were in any kind of trouble you'd tell me the truth, my boy, wouldn't you? All this worry has come through me. You're telling me the truth now, aren't you?'

'Yes, father.'

The older man smiled.

'Fathers have the privilege of asking "Are you a thief?" without having their heads punched! And most young people do stupid things—and most old people too! Lord! I once carried a quarter of a million bank at baccarat! Nobody would believe that, but it's true. Come and eat, then go along and see your Margot.'

'Father, who killed that man Wentford?'

There was a twinkle in McKay's eyes when he answered: 'J.G. Reeder, I should think. He knows more about it than any honest man should know!'

VIII. — REEDER—THE DEVIL

WHEN her visitor was gone, Ava opened the letter he had left with her, read a few lines of it, then threw letter and envelope into the fire. Funny, the sameness of men... they all wrote the same sort of stuff... raw stuff dressed up poetically... yet they thought they were being different from all other men. She did not resent these stereotypes of passion, nor did she feel sorry for those who used them. They were just normal experiences. She sat clasping her knees, her eyes on the fire. Then she got up dressed quickly and, going into Gower Street, found a cab.

She was set down at a house in an exclusive Mayfair street, and a liveried footman admitted her and told her there was company. There usually was in the early evening. She found twenty men and women sitting round a green table, watching a croupier with a large green shade over his eyes. He was turning up cards in two rows, and big monies, staked in compartments marked on the green table, went into the croupier's well or was pushed, with additions, to the fortunate winner.

The usual crowd, she noted. A pretty girl looked up and smiled then turned her eyes quickly and significantly to the young man by her side.

Ava found the governor in his room. He was smoking alone and reading the evening newspaper when she came in.

'Shut the door,' he ordered. 'What's wrong?'

'Nothing much. Only Feathers is bit worried.' She told him why.

Rufus Machfield smiled.

'Don't you worry, my pet,' he said kindly. 'There's been a murder down his way—did he tell you anything about that? I've just been reading about it. I should be surprised if old Reeder didn't get to the bottom of it—clever fellow, Reeder.'

He picked up his newspaper from the floor and his cigar from the ashtray where he had laid it.

'Rather a coincidence, wasn't it, Ava? Feathers pickin' on that account... Wentford's?'

She looked at him thoughtfully.

'Was it a coincidence?' she asked. 'That's what's worrying me. Did he pick on this poor man's account because he knew that he was going to be dead in a few days? I got a horrible creepy feeling when he was sitting beside me. I kept looking at his hands and wondering if there was blood on them!'

'Shuh!' said Machfield contemptuously. 'That rabbit!'

He opened a panel in the wall—it was nothing more romantic than a serving hatch when it was built—and glanced at the gamesters.

'They're playing for marbles!' he said in fine scorn. 'But they never do play high in the afternoon. Look at Lamontaine: he's bored sick.'

And certainly the croupier did not look happy. He closed the panel.

'I suppose you'll be raided one of these days?' she said.

'Sure!' he answered easily. 'But I've got another couple of houses ready for starting.'

'What do you think about Feathers? Will he squeal when they find him out?'

'Like a stuck pig,' said Machfield. 'He'll go down for nine months and get religion. That's the kind of fellow who gives the prison chaplain an interest in life. Ava, I've got a little job for you.'

She was alert, suspicious.

'Nothing much. I'll tell you all about it. Shall I open a bottle?'

'Yes, if it's milk,' she said. 'What's the little job and how much does it carry?'

'Would you faint if I said a thousand?' he asked, and opened the hatch again, looking through and closing it.

'Who are you expecting?' she asked. '... all right, don't be rude. No thousands never make me faint. Especially when they're talked about—'

'Now listen.'

Machfield was too good a talker to be brief. He led from a preamble to sections, into subsections...

'One minute.'

He interrupted his explanation to lift the hatch. She saw him bringing it down; then unexpectedly he raised it again. Was it the effect of odd lighting, or had his face changed colour? He dropped the hatch softly and gaped round at her.

'Who let him in? That doorman has "shopped" me—'

'Who is it?' she asked.

He beckoned her to his side, lifting the panel an inch.

'Stoop!' he hissed. 'Look... that fellow with the side-whiskers.'

'Oh—is he anybody?' She did not recognize the visitor. Possibly he was a bailiff; he looked hopelessly suburban, like the people who serve writs. They always wear ready-made ties and coloured handkerchiefs that stick out of their breast pockets.

'Reeder... J.G. Reeder!'

She wanted to raise the hatch and look, but he would not allow this.

'Go out and see what you can do... wait a bit.'

He lifted a house telephone and pressed a knob.

'Who was that fellow... the old fellow with side-whiskers? Got a card... what name... Reeder?'

He put down the phone unsteadily. Mr Machfield gave his membership cards to the right people. They were issued with the greatest care and after elaborate inquiries had been made as to the antecedents of the man or woman so honoured.

'Go and get acquainted... he doesn't know you. Go round through the buffet room and pretend you've just come in.'

When she reached the gaming room, Ava found Mr Reeder was sitting opposite the croupier. How he got that favoured chair was a mystery. His umbrella was between his knees. In front of him was a pile of banknotes. He was 'punting' gravely, seemingly absorbed in the game.

'Faîtes vos jeux, messieurs et mesdames,' said the croupier mechanically.

'What does he mean by that?' asked Mr Reeder of his nearest neighbour.

'He means "Make your bet",' said the girl, who had drawn up a chair by his side.

Mr Reeder made ten coups and won six pounds. With this he got up from the table and recovered his hat from beneath his chair.

'I always think that the time to—um—stop playing cards is when you're winning.' He imparted this truth to the young lady, who had withdrawn from the table at the same time.

'What a marvellous mind you have!' she said enthusiastically.

Mr Reeder winced.

'I'm afraid I have,' he said.

She shepherded him into the buffet room; he seemed quite willing to be refreshed at the expense of the house.

'A cup of tea, thank you, and a little seed cake.'

Ava was puzzled. Had the whole breed of busies undergone this shattering deterioration?

'I prefer seed to fruit cake,' he was saying. 'Curiously enough chickens are the same. I had a hen once—we called her Curly Toes—who could eat fruit and preferred it...'

She listened—she was a good listener. He offered to see her home.

'No—if you could drop me at the corner of Bruton Street and Berkeley Square—I don't live far from there,' she said modestly.

'Dear me!' said Mr Reeder, as he signalled a cab. 'Do you live in a mews too? So many people do.'

This was disconcerting.

'Perhaps you will come and see me one day—I am Mrs Coleforth- Ebling, and my phone number—do write this down—'

'My memory is very excellent,' murmured Mr Reeder.

The cab drove up at that moment and he opened the door.

'Ava Burslem—I will remember that—907, Gower Mansions.' He waved his hand in farewell as he got into the cab.

'I'll be seeing you again, my dear—toodle-oo!'

Mr Reeder could on occasions be outrageously frivolous. 'Toodle-oo!' was the high-water mark of his frivolity It was not remarkable that Ava was both alarmed and puzzled. Brighter intellects than hers had been shaken in a vain effort to reconcile Mr Reeder's appearance and manner with Mr Reeder's reputation.

She went back into the house and told Rufus Machfield what had happened.

'That man's clever,' said Machfield admiringly. 'If I were the man who had killed Wentworth or whatever his name is, I'd be shaking in my shoes. I'll walk round to the Leffingham and see if I can pick up a young game-fish. And you'd better dine with me, Ava—I'll give you the rest of the dope on that business I was discussing.'

The Leffingham Club was quite useful to Mr Machfield. It was a kind of potting shed where likely young shoots could be nurtured before being bedded out in the gardens of chance. Even Kenneth McKay had had his uses.

When Mr Reeder reached Scotland Yard, where they had arranged to meet, he found Inspector Gaylor charged with news.

'We've had a bit of luck!' he said. 'Do you remember those banknotes? You took their numbers... you remember? They were paid out on Wentford's account!'

'Oh, yes, yes, yes,' said Mr Reeder. 'To the veiled lady—'

'Veiled grandmother!' said Gaylor. 'We've traced two hundred pounds' worth to a moneylender. They were paid by Kenneth McKay, the bank clerk who cashed the cheque—and here's the cheque!'

He took it from a folder on his desk.

'The signature is a bad forgery; the cheque itself was not torn from Wentford cheque-book but from a book kept at the bank under McKay's charge!'

'Astounding!' said Mr. Reeder.

'Isn't it?' Mr Gaylor was smiling. 'So simple! I had the whole theory of the murders given me tonight. McKay forged and uttered the note, and to cover up his crime killed Wentford.'

'And you instantly arrested him?'

'Am I a child in arms?' asked Gaylor reproachfully. 'No, I questioned the lad. He doesn't deny that he paid the money lender, but says that the money came to him from some anonymous source. It arrived at his house by registered post. Poor young devil, he's terribly worried. What are we waiting for now?'

'A Gentleman Who Wants to Open a Box,' said Mr Reeder mysteriously.

'Reeder releases his mysteries as a miser pays his dentist,' said Gaylor to the superintendent. 'He knows I know all about the case—I admit he is very good and passes on most of the information he gets, but the old devil will keep back the connecting links!'

'Humour him,' said the superintendent.

IX. — TRAPPED!

MARGOT LYNN had spent a wretched and a weary day. The little city office which she occupied, and where she had conducted most of her uncle's business, had become a place of bad dreams.

She had never been very fond of her tyrannical relative who, if he had paid her well, had extracted the last ounce of service from her. He was an inveterate speculator, and had made considerable monies from his operations on the Stock Exchange. It was she who had bought and sold on his telephoned instructions, she who put his money into a London bank. Over her head all the time he had held one weapon: she had an invalid mother in Italy dependent on his charity.

All day long, people had been calling at the office. A detective had been there for two hours, taking a new statement; reporters had called in battalions, but these she had not seen. Mr Reeder had supplied her with an outer guard, a hard-faced woman who held the Pressmen at bay. But the police now knew everything there was to know about 'Wentford's' private affairs—except one thing. She was keeping faith with the dead in this respect, though every time she thought of her reservation her heart sank.

She finished her work and went home, leaving the building by a back door to avoid the patient reporters. They were waiting for her at her flat, but the hard-faced Mrs Grible swept them away.

Once safely in the flat, a difficulty arose. How could she tactfully and delicately dismiss the guard which Mr Reeder had provided? She offered the woman tea, and Mrs Grible, who said very little, embarrassed her by making it.

'I'm greatly obliged to you and Mr Reeder,' she said after the little meal. 'I don't think I ought to take up any more of your time—'

'I'm staying until Mr Reeder comes,' said the lady.

Very meekly the girl accepted the situation.

Mr Reeder did not come until ten o'clock. Margot was half dead with weariness, and would have given her legacy to have undressed and gone to bed.

For his part, he was in the liveliest mood, an astounding circumstance remembering that he had had practically no sleep for thirty-six hours. In an indefinable way he communicated to her some of his own vitality. She found herself suddenly very wide awake.

'You have seen the police, of course?' Mr Reeder sat on a chair facing her, leaning on the handle of his umbrella, his hat carefully deposited on the floor by his side. 'And you have told them everything? It is very wise. The key, now—did you tell them about the key?'

She went very red. She was—thought Mr Reeder—almost as pretty when she was red as when she was white.

'The key?' She could fence, a little desperately, with the question, although she knew just what he meant.

'At the cottage last night you showed me two keys—one the key of the house, the other, from shape and make, the key of a safe deposit.'

Margot nodded.

'Yes. I suppose I should have told them that. But Mr Wentford—'

'Asked you never to tell. That is why he had two keys, one for you and one for himself.'

'He hated paying taxes—' she began.

'Did he ever come up to London?'

'Only on very wet and foggy days. I've never been to the safe deposit, Mr Reeder. Anything that is there he placed himself. I only had the key in case of accidents.'

'What was he afraid of—did he ever tell you?'

She shook her head.

'He was terribly afraid of something. He did all his own housework and cooking—he would never have anybody in. A gardener used to come every few days and look after the electric light plant, and Mr Wentford used to pay him through the window. He was afraid of bombs—you've seen the cage round the window in his bedroom? He had that put there for fear somebody should throw in a bomb while he was asleep. I can't tell you what precautions he took. Except myself and the policeman, and once Mr Enward the lawyer, nobody has ever entered that house. His laundry was put outside the door every week and left at the door. He had an apparatus for testing milk and he analysed every drop that was left at the door before he drank it—he practically lived on milk. It wasn't so bad when I first went to him —I was sixteen then—but it got worse and worse as the years went on.'

'He had two telephones in the house,' said Mr Reeder. 'That was rather extravagant.'

'He was afraid of being cut off. The second one was connected by underground wires—it cost him an awful lot of money.' She heaved a deep, relieved sigh. 'Now I've told everything, and my conscience is clear. Shall I get the keys?'

'They are for Mr Gaylor,' said Mr Reeder hastily. 'I think you had better keep them and give them to nobody else. Not even to the person who calls tonight.'

'Who is calling tonight?' she asked.

Mr Reeder avoided the question. He looked at Mrs Grible, grim and silent.

'Would you mind—er—waiting outside?'

The obedient woman melted from the room.

'There is one point we ought to clear up, my dear young friend,' said Mr Reeder in a hushed voice. 'How long had you been in your uncle's house when Mr Kenneth McKay appeared?'

If he had struck her she could not have wilted as she did. Her face went the colour of chalk, and she dropped into a chair.

'He came through the window into the little lobby? I know all about that—but how long after you arrived?'

She tried to speak twice before she succeeded.

'A few minutes,' she said, not raising her eyes.

Then suddenly, she sprang up.

'He knew nothing about the murder—he was stupidly jealous and followed me... and then I explained to him, and he believed me... I looked through the window and saw you and told him to go... that is the truth, I swear it is!'

He patted her gently on the shoulder.

'I know it is the truth, my dear—be calm, I beg of you. That is all I wanted to know.'

He called Mrs Grible by name. As she came in, they heard the bell of the front door ring. It was followed by a gentle rat-tat.

'Who would that be?' asked Margot. She was still trembling.

'It may be a reporter—it may not be.' Mr Reeder rose. 'If it is some stranger to see you on urgent business, perhaps you would be kind enough to mention the fact that you are quite alone.'

He looked helplessly round.

'That—' He pointed to a door.

'Is the kitchen,' she said, hardly noticing his embarrassment.

'Very excellent.' He was relieved. Opening the door, he waved Mrs Grible to precede him. 'If it should be reporters we will deal with them,' he said, and closed the door behind him.

There was a second ring of the bell as Margot hurried to the door. Standing outside was a girl. She was elegantly dressed, was a little older than Margot, and pretty.

'Can I see you, Miss Lynn? It's rather important.' Margot hesitated.

'Come in, please,' she said at last. The girl followed her into the sitting-room. 'All alone?' she said lightly. Margot nodded.

'You're a great pal of Kenneth's, aren't you?' She saw the colour come into Margot's face, and laughed.

'Of course you are—and you've had an awful row?'

'I've had no awful row,' said Margot quietly.

'Well, he's a darling boy, and he's in terrible trouble.'

'Trouble—what kind of trouble?' asked Margot quickly.

'Police trouble—'

The girl swayed and caught at the back of a chair.

'Don't get upset!' Ava was enjoying her part. 'He'll be able to explain everything—'

'But he said he believed me...' She was on the point of betraying the presence of the hidden Mr Reeder, but checked herself in time.

'Who said so?' asked Ava curiously. 'A copper—policeman, I mean? Don't take any notice of that kind of trash. They'd lie to save a car fare! We know that Kenneth didn't forge the cheque—'

Margot's eyes opened wide in amazement.

'Forge a cheque—what do you mean? I don't understand what you're talking about.'

For a moment Ava was nonplussed. If this girl did not know about the forgery, what was agitating her? The solution of this minor mystery came in a flash. It was the murder! Kenneth was in it! She went cold at the thought.

'Oh, my God! I didn't think of that!' she gasped.

'Tell me about this forgery—' began Margot, and her visitor remembered her errand.

'I want you to come along and see Kenneth. He's waiting for you at my flat—naturally he can't come here. He'll tell you everything.'

Margot was bewildered.

'Of course I'll come, but—'

'Don't "but," my dear—just slip into your things and come along. Kenneth told me to ask you to bring all the keys you have—he said they can prove his innocence—'

'Dear, dear, dear!' said a gentle voice, and Ava flung round, to face the man who had come into the room.

She was trapped and knew it. That old devil!

'The key of the larder now, would that be of any use to you?' asked Mr Reeder in his jocular mood. 'Or the key of Wormwood Scrubs?'

'Hullo, Reeder!' The girl was coolness itself. 'I thought you were alone, Miss Lynn. I didn't know you were entertaining Mr and Mrs Reeder.'

Such an outrageous statement made Mr Reeder blush, but it did not confuse him. Nor did Mrs Grible seem particularly distressed.

'This lady is Mrs Grible, of my department,' he said gravely.

'She must have some use,' said Ava. She picked up her coat which she had taken off. 'I'll phone you later, Miss Lynn.'

'The cells at Bow Street police station are hygienically equipped, but they have no telephones,' said Mr Reeder, and for the first time in many years Ava lost her nerve.

'What's the idea—cells?' she demanded loudly. 'You've got nothing on me—'

'We shall see—will you step this way?' He opened the door of the kitchen. 'I should like to have a few words with you.'

He heard a knock at the outer door and looked at Margot.

'I shall be on hand,' he said.

She went to the door—and stepped back at the sight of her visitor. It was Kenneth McKay. He looked at her gravely, and without a word took her into his arms and kissed her. He had never kissed her that way before.

'Can I see you?'

She nodded and took him back to her room. The other three had disappeared.

'It is only right that you should know, darling, that I'm in terrible trouble. I've just come from home, and I suppose the police are after me. They may be after my father, too. He knew Wentford—hated him. I didn't dream that—'

'Ken—what about you? Why do the police want you?'

He looked at her steadily.

'It's about a forged cheque. Some of the money has been traced to me. Darling, I've come to ask you something, and I want you to tell me the truth. Kingfether as good as told me I was a liar when I said I'd cashed it for a veiled woman. I don't mind really what he says—he's a crook, that fellow! Money has been missing from the bank—they sent old Reeder down weeks ago—'

'How did they trace money to you?' she interrupted. 'And what do you want me to tell you?'

'You knew that I owed money—I told you.' She nodded. 'And how worried I was about it. I can't remember whether I told you how much I owed—'

She shook her head.

'You didn't,' she said, and he drew a long breath.

'Then it wasn't you,' he said.

He described the arrival of the letter containing the bank notes.

'Two hundred pounds, and of course I wanted the money badly.'

'Who else knew that you were short of money?' she asked.

'Oh, everybody.' He was in despair. 'I talked about it—Kingfether said that he never ordered me to cash any cheque that came, and that the story of a veiled woman arriving by car from London when he was out at lunch was all moonshine—hullo!'

He saw the door of the kitchen opening and gasped at the sight of Mr Reeder.

'It wasn't moonshine, my young friend,' said Mr Reeder. 'In fact, I—er—have interviewed a garage keeper who filled up the tank of the lady's car, and incidentally saw the lady.'

He turned to the room and beckoned Ava. Kenneth stared at her.

'Well?' she said defiantly. 'Do you think you'll know me again?'

'I know you now!' he said huskily. 'You're the woman who cashed the cheque!'

'That's a damned lie!' she screamed.

'S-sh!' said Mr Reeder, shocked.

'I've never seen him before!' she added, and Margot gasped.

'But you told me—'

'I've never seen him before,' insisted the woman.

'You'll see him again,' said Mr Reeder gently. 'You on one side—the wrong side—of the witness box, and he on the other!'

Then she lost her head.

'If there was a swindle, he was in it!' she said, speaking rapidly. 'You don't suppose any clerk would pay out six hundred pounds to somebody he'd never seen before unless he had his instructions and got his corner! How did I know the cheque was forged? It seemed all right to me.'

'May it continue to seem all right,' said Mr Reeder piously. 'May you be consoled through the long period of your incarceration with the—er—comfort of a good conscience. I think you'll get three years—but if your previous convictions influence the judge, I fancy you'll get five!'

Ava collapsed.

'You can't charge me,' she whimpered. 'I didn't forge anything.'

'There is a crime called "uttering",' said Mr Reeder. '"Uttering—knowing to be forged." Will you take the young lady's arm, Mrs Grible? I will take the other—probably we shall meet a policeman en route. And did I say anything about "conspiracy"? That is also an offence. Mind that mat, Mrs Grible.'

X. — THE RAID

THERE was some rather heavy play at Mr Machfield's private establishment—heavier than usual, and this gave the proprietor of the house cause for uneasiness. If Mr Reeder had reported his visit that afternoon to the police, and they thought the moment expedient, there would be a raid tonight, and in preparation for this all doors leading to the mews at the back were unfastened, and a very powerful car was waiting. Machfield might or might not use that method of escape. On the other hand, he could follow his invariable practice, which was to appear among those present as a guest: a fairly simple matter, because he was not registered as the proprietor of the house; indeed the premises were unlicensed, which was the cause of his fear.

Certainly the car would have its uses, if everything went right and there was no untoward incident. Just lately, however, there had been one or two little hitches in the smooth running of his affairs and, being superstitious, he expected more.

He looked at his watch; his appointment with Ava was at midnight, but she had promised to phone through before then. At a quarter to nine, as he stood watching the players there came a newcomer at the tail of three others. He was wearing a dinner jacket, as were the majority of people round the board, and he looked strangely out of place in those surroundings, though his blue chin was newly shaved and his black hair was glossy.

Mr Machfield watched him wander aimlessly around the table, and then caught his eye and indicated that he wished to see him. Soon afterwards he walked out of the room and Mr Kingfether followed.

'You're rather silly to come tonight, K,' said Mr Machfield. 'There's just a chance of a raid—Reeder was here this afternoon.'

The manager's jaw dropped.

'Is he here now?' he asked, and Mr Machfield smiled at the foolishness of the question.

'No, and he won't be coming tonight, unless he arrives with a flying squad. We'll keep that bird out at any rate'

'Where's Ava?' asked Kingfether.

'She'll be in later,' lied Machfield. 'She had a bit of a headache, and I advised her not to come.'

The bank manager helped himself to a whisky from a decanter on the sideboard.

'I'm very fond of that girl,' said Kingfether.

'Who isn't?' asked the other.

'To me'—there was a tremor in the younger man's voice—'she is something outside of all my experience. Do you think she's fond of me, Machfield?'

'I'm sure she is,' said the other heartily; 'but she's a woman of the world, you know, my boy, and women of the world don't carry their hearts on their sleeves.'

He might have added that, in the case of Ava, she carried the business equivalent of that organ up her sleeve, ready for exhibition to any susceptible man, young or old.

'Do you think she'd marry me, Machfield?'

Machfield did not laugh. He had played cards a great deal and had learned to school his countenance. Ava had two husbands, and had not gone through the formality of freeing her self from either. Both were officially abroad, the foreign country being that stretch of desolate moorland which lies between Ashburton and Tavistock. Here, in the gaunt convict establishment of Princetown, they laboured for the good of their souls, but with little profit to the taxpayers who supported them, and even supplied them with tobacco.

'Why shouldn't she? But mind, she's an expensive kind of girl, K,' said Machfield very seriously. 'She costs a lot of money to dress, and you'd have to find it from somewhere—fifteen hundred a year doesn't go far with a girl who buys her clothes in Paris.'

Kingfether strode up and down the apartment, his hands in his pockets, his head on his chest, a look of gloom on a face that was never touched with brightness.

'I realize that,' he said, 'but if she loved me she'd help to make both ends meet. I've got to cut out this business of the bank; I've had a fright, and I can't take the risk again. In fact, I thought of leaving the bank and setting up a general agency in London.'

Machfield knew what a general agency was when it was run by an inexperienced man. An office to which nobody came except bill collectors. He didn't, however, wish to discourage his client; for the matter of that, Kingfether gave him little opportunity for comment.

'There's going to be hell's own trouble about that cheque,' he said. 'I had a letter from head office—I have to report to the general manager in the morning and take McKay with me. That's the usual course.'

Such details were distasteful to Mr Machfield. He needed all the spare room in his mind for other matters much more weighty than the routine of the Great Central Bank, but he was more than interested in the fate of McKay.

Kingfether came back to Ava, because Ava filled his horizon.

'The first time I ever met her,' he said, 'I knew she was the one woman in the world for me. I know she's had a rough time and that she's had a battle to live. But who am I to judge?'

'Who, indeed?' murmured Mr Machfield, with considerable truth. And then, pursuing his thought, 'What will happen to Mr Kenneth McKay?'

Only for a moment did the manager look uncomfortable.

'He is not my concern,' he said loudly. 'There's no doubt at all that the signature on the cheque—'

'Oh, yes, yes,' said the other impatiently. 'We don't want to discuss that, do we? I mean, not between friends. You paid me the money you owed me, and there was an end to it so far as I am concerned. I took a bit of a risk myself, sending Ava down—I mean, letting Ava go,' he corrected, when he saw the look on the other's face. 'What about young McKay?'

The manager shrugged his shoulders.

'I don't know and I really don't care. When I got back to the bank this afternoon he'd gone, though I'd left instructions that he was to stay until I returned. Of course, I can't report it, because I did wrong to go away myself, and it was rather awkward that one of our bank inspectors called when I was out. I shall have to work all night to make up arrears. McKay might have helped me. In fact, I told him—'

'Oh, he came back, did he?'

'For five minutes, just before six o'clock. He just looked in and went out again. That's how I knew the inspector had called. I had to tell this pup about the cheque and the banknotes. By the way, that's a mystery to me how the notes came into his hands at all—I suppose there's no mistake about them? If he was in the habit of coming here he might have got them from the table. He doesn't come here, does he?'

'Not often.' Machfield might have added that nobody came to that place unless they had a certain amount of surplus wealth, or the means by which easy money could be acquired.

There were quite a number of his clients who were in almost exactly the same position as Mr Kingfether—people in positions of trust, men who had the handling of other people's money. It was no business of Machfield's how that money was obtained, so long as it was judiciously spent. It was his boast that his game was straight; as indeed it was—up to a point. He had allowed himself throughout life a certain margin of dishonesty, which covered both bad luck and bad investments. Twice in his life he had gone out for big coups. Once he had failed, the other time he had succeeded but had made no money.

He was not persona grata in all the countries of the world. If he had arrived at Monte Carlo he would have left by very nearly the next train, or else the obliging police would have placed a car at his disposal to take him across to Nice, a resort which isn't so particular about the character of her temporary visitors.

'I'm sorry for McKay in a way, but it's a case of his life or mine, Machfield. Either he goes down or I go down—and I'm not going down.'

Nothing wearied Machfield worse than heroics. And yet he should have been hardened to them, for he had lived in an atmosphere of hectic drama, and once had seen a victim of his lying dead by his own hand across the green board of his gaming table. But it was years ago.

'You'd better slide back to the room,' he said. 'I'll come in a little later. Don't play high: I've still got some of your papers, dear boy.'

When he returned to the room, the manager had found a seat at the table and was punting modestly and with some success. The croupier asked a question with a flick of his eyelids, and almost imperceptibly Machfield shook his head, which meant that that night, at any rate, Kingfether would pay for his losses in cash, that neither his IOUs nor cheques would be accepted.

From time to time the players got up from the tables, strolled into the buffet, had a drink and departed. But there was always a steady stream of newcomers to take their places. Mr Machfield went back to his study, for he was expecting a telephone message. It came at a quarter past ten. A woman's voice said: 'Ava says everything is OK.'

He replaced the telephone with a smile. Ava was a safe bet: you could always trust that girl, and he did not question her ability to keep her visitor occupied for at least two hours. After that he would do a little questioning himself. But it must be he, and not that other fool.

Kingfether was winning; there was a big pile of pound and five-pound notes before him. He looked animated, and for once in his life pleased. The bank was winning too; there was a big box recessed into the table, and this was full of paper money and every few minutes the pile was augmented.

A dull evening! Mr Machfield would be glad when the time came to put on his record of the National Anthem. He always closed down on this patriotic note; it left the most unlucky of players with the comforting sense that at least they had their country left to them.

He was looking at the long folding door of the room as it opened slowly. It was second nature in him to watch that opening door, and until this moment he had never been shocked or startled by what it revealed. Now, however, he stood dumbfounded, for there was Mr Reeder, without his hat, and even without his umbrella.

Nobody noticed him except the proprietor, and he was frozen to the spot. With an apologetic smile Mr Reeder came tiptoeing across to him.

'Do you very much mind?' he asked in an urgent whisper. 'I find time hanging rather heavily on my hands.'

Machfield licked his dry lips.

'Come here, will you?'

He went back to his study, Reeder behind him.

'Now, Mr Reeder, what's the idea of your coming here? How did you get in? I gave strict instructions to the man on the door—'

'I told him a lie,' said Mr Reeder in a hushed tone, as though the enormity of his offence had temporarily overcome him. 'I said that you had particularly asked me to come to night. That was very wrong, and I am sorry. The truth is, Mr Machfield, even the most illustrious of men have their little weaknesses; even the cleverest and most law-abiding their criminal instincts, and although I am neither illustrious nor clever, I have the frailties of my—er—humanity. Not, I would add, that it is criminal to play cards for money—far from it. I, as you probably know, or you may have heard, have a curiously distorted mind. I find my secret pleasures in such places as these.'

Mr Machfield was relieved, immensely relieved. He knew detectives who gambled, but somehow he had never associated Mr J.G. Reeder with this peculiar weakness.

'Why, certainly, we're glad to see you, Mr Reeder,' he said heartily.

He was so glad indeed that he would have been happy to have given this odd-looking man the money wherewith to play.

'You'll have a drink on the house—not,' he added quickly, 'that I am in any position to offer you a drink. I am a guest the same as yourself, but I know the proprietor would be annoyed if you came and went without having one.'

'I never drink. A little barley water perhaps?'

There was, unfortunately, no barley water in the establishment, but this, as Machfield explained, would be remedied in the future—even now if he wished. Mr Reeder, however, would not hear of putting 'the house' to trouble. He was anxious to join the company, and again by some extraordinary quality of good luck, he managed to insinuate himself so that he sat opposite the croupier. Somebody rose from their chair as he approached, and Mr Reeder took the vacant seat.

He might have taken a chair on the opposite side of the table, for at the sight of him a pallid Kingfether had whipped out his handkerchief and covered the lower part of his face as though he were suffering from a bad cold.

Stealthily he rose from his seat and melted into the fringe of people standing behind the players.

'Don't let me drive you away, Mr Kingfether,' said Reeder—and everybody heard him.

The manager dropped back till he stood against the wall, a limp helpless figure, and there he remained through the scene that followed.

Mr Reeder had produced a bundle of banknotes which he counted with great care. It was not a big bundle. Mr Machfield, watching, guessed he was in the ten-pound line of business, and certainly there was no more than that on the table.

One by one those little notes of Reeder's disappeared, until there was nothing left, and then a surprising thing happened. Mr. Reeder put his hand in his pocket, groped painfully and produced something which he covered with his hand. The croupier had raised his cards ready to deal—the game was trente-et-quarante—when the interruption came.

'Excuse me.' J.G. Reeder's voice was gentle but everybody it the table heard it. 'You can't play with that pack: there are two cards missing.'

The croupier raised his head. The green-shade strapped to his glossy head threw a shadow which hid the top half of his face.

He stared blandly at the interrupter—the dispassionate and detached stare which only a professional croupier can give.

'Pardon?' he said, puzzled. 'I do not understand, m'sieur. The pack is complete. It is never questioned—'

'There are two cards without which I understand you cannot play your game,' said Mr Reeder, and suddenly lifted his hand.

On the table before him were two playing cards, the ace of diamonds and the ace of hearts. The croupier looked down at them, and then, with an oath, pushed back his chair and dropped his hand to his hip.

'Don't move—I beg of you.'

There was an automatic in Mr Reeder's hand, and its muzzle was directed towards the croupier's white waistcoat. 'Ladies and gentlemen, there is nothing to be alarmed about. Stand back from the table against the wall, and do not come between me and Monsieur Lamontaine!'

He himself stepped backward.

'Over there!' he signalled to Machfield.

'Look here, Reeder—'

'Over there!' snarled J.G. Reeder. 'Stand up by your friend. Ladies and gentlemen,'—he addressed the company again without taking his eyes from the croupier—' this establishment is not licensed. Your names and addresses will be taken, but I will use my best endeavours to avoid police court proceedings, because we are after something much more important than that.'

And then the guests saw strange men standing in the doorway. They came from all directions—from Machfield's study, from the hall below, from the roof above. They handcuffed Lamontaine and took away the two guns he carried, one in each hip pocket—Machfield was unarmed.

'What will the charge be?'

'Mr Gaylor will tell you that at the police station. But I think the question is unnecessary. Honestly, don't you, Mr Machfield?'

Machfield said nothing.

XI. — DEDUCTION

MR REEDER kept what he called a casebook, in which he inscribed passionless accounts of all the cases in which he was engaged. Some of these cases had no value except to the technician, and would not interest anyone except perhaps the psychopathologist. Under the heading 'Two Aces' appeared this account, written in his own handwriting.

Ten years ago,—wrote Mr Reeder—there arrived at the Hotel Majestic in Nice a man who described himself in the hotel register as Rufus Machfield. He had a number of other names, but it is only necessary that Machfield should be used to identify this particular character. The man had a reputation as a cardsharp and, in the pursuit of his nefarious calling, had 'worked' the ships plying between England and New York. He had also been convicted on two occasions as a professional gambler in Germany.

He was of Danish origin, but at the time was a naturalized Englishman, with a permanent address in Colvin Gardens, Bayswater. At the Majestic Hotel he had met with Charles or Walter Lynn, an adventurer who had also 'operated' the ships on the North Atlantic. On one of these trips Lynn had become acquainted with Mr George McKay, a prosperous woollen merchant of Bradford. There is no evidence that they ever played cards together, and Mr McKay does not recall that they did. But the friendship was of value to Lynn because Mr McKay was in the habit of coming to Nice every year, and was in residence at the time Lynn and Machfield met. McKay was known as a resolute and successful gambler, and before now had figured in sensational play.

The two men, Lynn and Machfield, conferred together and decided on a scheme to rob McKay at the tables. Gambling in Nice is not confined to the recognized establishments. There was at the time a number of Cercles Privés where play was even higher than at the public rooms, and the most reputable of these was 'Le Signe' which, if it was not recognized, was winked at by the French authorities.

In order to swindle McKay, a patron of this club, it was necessary to secure the co-operation and help of an official. Lynn's choice fell on a young croupier named Lamontaine, and he in turn was to suborn two other croupiers, both of whom it was intended should receive a very generous share of the money.

Lamontaine proved to be a singularly pliable tool. He had married a young wife and had got into debt, and he was fearful that this should come to the ears of the club authorities. An interview was arranged in Lyons; the scheme was put before the croupier by Lynn, and he agreed to come in, taking a half share for himself and his two fellow croupiers, the other half being equally divided between Lynn and Machfield. Lynn apparently demurred at the division, but Machfield was satisfied with his quarter share; the more so as he knew McKay had been winning very heavily, and providing he had the right kind of betting, there would be a big killing.

The game to be played was baccarat, for McKay could never resist the temptation of taking a bank, especially a big bank. It was very necessary that arrangements should be hurried on before the merchant left the South of France, and a fortnight after the preliminaries, Lamontaine reported that everything was in trim, that he had secured the co-operation of his comrades, and it was decided that the coup should be brought off on the Friday night.

It was arranged that Lynn should be the player, and that after play was finished the conspirators should meet again at Lyons, when the loot was to be divided. The cards were to be stacked so that the bank won every third coup. It was arranged that the signal for the conspirators to begin their betting was to be the dealing of two aces, the ace of diamonds and the ace of hearts. Somebody would draw a six to these, and the banker would have a 'natural'—which means, I understand, that he would win.

Thereafter the betting was to be done by Lynn, and the first was a banco call—which meant, as the card lay, that the bank would be swept into their pockets. They knew McKay would bid for the bank, but they would bid higher, and Lynn then took the bank with a capital of a million francs. Fourteen times the bank won, and had now reached enormous proportions, so much so that every other table in the room was deserted, and the table where this high play was going on was surrounded by curious watchers.

There were fourteen winning coups for the bank, and the amount gathered up at the finish by Lynn was something in the neighbourhood of £400,000. Lamontaine states that it was more, but Machfield is satisfied that it was in that region. The money was taken to the hotel, and the following night Lynn left for Lyons. He was to be joined the next day by Machfield, and on the Sunday they were to meet the croupier in Paris and pay him his share.

The night that Lynn left, however, one of the officials of the rooms made a statement to his chief. He had lost his nerve and he betrayed his comrades. Lamontaine, with the other croupier, was arrested on a charge of conspiracy, and Machfield only got away from the South of France by the skin of his teeth. He journeyed on to Lyons and arrived there in the early hours of the following afternoon. He hoped that no news of the arrests would have got into the papers and scared his partner; and certainly he did not wire warning Lynn. When he got to the hotel he asked for his friend, but was told that he had not arrived, nor had he made a reservation of the rooms which had been agreed upon.

From that moment he disappeared from human ken, and neither Machfield nor any of his friends were able to trace him. It was no accident: it was a deliberate double-cross.

Machfield played the game as far as he was able, and when he was released from prison and came to Paris, a broken man, for his young wife had died while he was in gaol, he helped the croupier as well as he could, and together they came to England to establish gaming-houses, but primarily to find Lynn and force him to disgorge.

There was another person on the track of Lynn. McKay, who had been robbed, as he knew after the French court proceedings, employed me to trace him, but for certain reasons I was unable to justify his confidence.

I do not know in what year or month Lamontaine and Machfield located their man. It is certain that 'Mr Wentford,' as he called himself, lived in increasing fear of their vengeance. When they did locate him he proved to be an impossible man to reach. I have no doubt that the house was carefully reconnoitred, his habits studied, and that attempts were made to get at him. But those attempts failed. It is highly probable, though no proof of this exists, that he was well informed as to his enemy's movements, for so far as can be gathered from the statement of his niece and checked by the admissions of Machfield, Lynn never left his house except on the days when Machfield and Lamontaine were in Paris—they frequently went to that city over the week-end.

It was Lamontaine who formed the diabolical plan which was eventually to lead to Wentford's death. He knew that the only man admitted to the house was the policeman who patrolled that part of the country, so he studied police methods, even got information as to the times on which the beat was patrolled, and on the night of the murder, soon after it was dark, he travelled down to Beaconsfield by car through the storm, accompanied by Machfield.

Lamontaine at some time or other had been on the French stage—he spoke perfect English—and I have no doubt was in a position to make himself up sufficiently well to deceive Wentford into opening the door. At seven o'clock Constable Verity left the station and proceeded on his patrol. At seven-thirty he was ruthlessly murdered by a man who stepped out of hiding and shot him point-blank through the heart.

The body was taken into a field and laid out, the two murderers hoping that the snow would cover it. Lamontaine was already wearing the uniform of a police constable and, mounting the motorbike, he rode on to Wentford's house. The old man saw him through the window, and, suspecting nothing, got down and opened the door.

He may not have realized that anything was wrong until he was back in his parlour, for it was there that he was struck down. The two men intended leaving him in the cottage, but a complication arose while they were searching the place, or endeavouring to open the safe behind the bookcase. The telephone rang, one of them answered in a disguised voice and heard Margot Lynn say that she was coming on but was delayed.

The thing to do now was to remove the body. Lifting it out, they laid it over the motorcycle and, guiding the machine down to the road, pushed it towards Beaconsfield. Here a second complication arose: the lights of Mr Enward's car were seen coming toward them. The body was dropped by the side of the road, and the constable took his place on the bike. The seat was smothered with the blood of the murdered man, and Mr Enward's clerk must have quite innocently rubbed his sleeve against it, for it was afterwards discovered that his coat was stained. That gave me my first clue, and I was able, owing to my peculiar mind, to reconstruct the crime as it had been committed.

The two men joined one another again in the vicinity of the cottage. They were not able to make any further attempt that night. One of them, however, heard that the girl knew where the money was cached. I am afraid I was responsible for this, and it was intended that she should be taken away, with the key of the safe deposit...

Machfield had already become acquainted with the straightened circumstances of young McKay, the son of his victim, and probably to hit at his father, who he must have known was still hunting for him, used an opportunity which was offered by chance, to ruin him, as he believed.

Two hundred pounds, representing a portion of the money obtained from the bank by a fraudulent manager (3 years Prison; Central Criminal Court) through the instrumentality of his woman friend (5 years: CCC) was sent anonymously to the younger McKay by Machfield, and was traced to the young man.

After this came a note, also in Mr Reeder's hand:

'Rufus John Machfield and Antonio Lamontaine (sentence: death, CCC) executed at Wandsworth Prison, April 17th. Executioner Ellis.'

Mr Reeder was a stickler for facts.

Printed in Great Britain
by Amazon